CW01213185

UNIFORMED CABAL

CONNOR WHITELEY

No part of this book may be reproduced in any form or by any electronic or mechanical means. Including information storage, and retrieval systems, without written permission from the author except for the use of brief quotations in a book review.

This book is NOT legal, professional, medical, financial or any type of official advice.

Any questions about the book, rights licensing, or to contact the author, please email connorwhiteley@connorwhiteley.net

Copyright © 2024 CONNOR WHITELEY

All rights reserved.

DEDICATION

Thank you to all my readers without you I couldn't do what I love.

PROLOGUE
9th November 2023
Canterbury, England

His life was about to change and he was going to get the beating of his life.

Detective Kinsley loved his job as a detective for Kent Police. He got to help the innocent, protect them and he got to put evil people away, but he had never ever expected things to turn this bad.

Kinsley went up a very long road with freshly laid black tarmacking, he was glad the local council had finally decided to fix the potholes along here. He flicked a look at each of the large, white, modern semi-detached houses as he went.

Kinsley didn't see anything too interesting in the houses. It was late at night and everything was coloured with the faint yellow light coming from the nearby streetlights but all the curtains seemed to be drawn shut, not a single car was driving about and no one was outside.

The faint aromas of chestnuts, spices and pumpkins filled the air leaving the taste of lightly spiced pumpkin lattes on his tongue, it was probably from someone's dinner and Kinsley would have loved to have been at home with his boyfriend eating dinner together, but this was too important.

He kept going up the road because he had to give vital information to his friend and the only woman he trusted. He had to speak to Bettie English before he was killed.

He couldn't let this information get into the wrong hands.

Kinsley had always been aware of police corruption, it was plain as day within the force, and he had always been too much of a coward to stand up against it. But this was different.

Kinsley heard a car slowly start to drive up behind him.

He had learnt of a top-secret cabal within Kent Police that abused its power, gave powerful positions to corrupt officers and they were corrupting the police force right up to the highest levels.

Kinsley had proof of it and he knew every single member of the cabal. It was only five people but they were so powerful, clever and influential that the Cabal didn't need anymore.

The car behind him got closer and closer.

Kinsley went quicker and quicker.

He had to get to Bettie English and give her the memory stick. There was nothing more important in the entire world.

A crowbar smashed into Kinsley's head.

He collapsed down to the ground and just saw a man and woman dressed in black lift up the crowbar and bought it down on him.

Again and again.

Until his world went black.

CHAPTER 1
10th November 2023
Canterbury, England

Private Eye Bettie English had always loved going out for early breakfast with her nephew, his boyfriend and her two little angels, Harrison and Elizabeth who just sat in their high chairs at the large square wooden table and just talked to each other about random colours and things they saw.

Bettie loved her kids more than anything else in the entire world and she loved her family. They were amazing.

She pulled in her warm metal chair a little bit more and rested her arms on the even warmer wooden table in the café she was in. Each of them had a large white mug of coffee and the two kids had some baby formula in a blue and pink bottle next to them.

Bettie had to admit this café did the most amazing pumpkin-spiced lattes ever. Even now she could smell the sweet spicy delights of the spices, the caramel and the sugar that made the great taste of pumpkin pie form on her tongue. She loved drinking here.

They had just ordered and Bettie smiled at her nephew Sean with his tasteful and very stylishly done pink highlights in his long blond hair, as he sat next to his boyfriend Harry. They were both wearing black jeans and trainers and a fake golden watch they had bought each other as a gaff gift for Halloween (Bettie still had no idea why) but she had to admit Sean's light pink hoody looked great. And it was a nice contrast to Harry's black one.

They were talking, smiling and whispering to each other like they were concocting some evil plan for the rest of the day. Bettie was never going to deny how cute of a couple they made.

She was a little surprised how empty the café was. Normally there was a long line of elderly women, middle-aged men and young families like Bettie against the orange brick wall on the far side. But the line was tiny today.

The rows upon rows of square wooden tables were almost empty but there was a largeish group of young mothers sitting behind them that Bettie had spotted them. They were singing quietly and just talking to their kids.

Bettie had wanted to laugh at the types of things they were talking about with their kids but Bettie had little doubt they were great mothers.

"What you ordering auntie?" Sean asked.

Bettie was about to answer as a large group of men and women walking past the hug floor-to-ceiling windows a few rows over caught her eye.

"I heard there's a protest further up the high street today," Harry said.

"What about?" Bettie asked really wanting to know if there was a potential case for her to help with.

"Mummy look," Elizabeth said.

Bettie just laughed as she saw that somehow Harrison had popped off the lid of his bottle and thrown his milk over his sister.

"Don't do that," Bettie said to Harrison with a warning finger.

The little one didn't look happy but as the three adults dried up Elizabeth, Bettie gestured Harry to continue.

"Something about police corruption and the unfair dismissal of a young officer," Harry said.

Bettie rolled her eyes. She was trying not to think about the damn police right now because this was the final day of her boyfriend, Detective Graham Adams' police misconduct hearing.

It was a complete kangaroo court that was fixed to get him out of the police because he was always exposing police corruption, showing up lazy officers and more but Bettie couldn't do too much to help him.

She might have been President of the British

Private Eye Federation, an organisation that had more power than the governments of most small countries, but when it came to internal policing matters she had no power.

And she hated it.

Bettie kissed Elizabeth on the head and looked at Harrison when her phone buzzed.

"Apologise to your sister," Bettie said.

"Sorry," Harrison said trying to give his sister a kiss but he was strapped into the highchair too well.

"Good boy," Bettie said looking at her phone.

She was missed that it was from her assistant Fran and she wanted Bettie to call her.

"Big problem," Fran said as soon as she answered. "Detective Kinsley was beaten within an inch of his life last night two blocks away from yours,"

Bettie just gasped. She couldn't think of anything to say.

Bettie couldn't believe someone would actually attack Kinsley, he was such a nice guy, a good cop and he was a great man. Why the hell would anyone want to attack him?

"I have to ask Bet," Fran said, "did you see him last night?"

"What's going on?" Bettie asked knowing Fran wouldn't be asking questions without good reason.

"Because Bettie when the paramedics eventually found Kinsley he was only saying two words. *Bettie Federation*,"

"He wanted to see me," Bettie said. "Where is he? I have to talk to him,"

"Impossible. He's in a medically induced coma at Canterbury Hospital because of swelling on the brain,"

"I'm at Lotts' Cafe," Bettie said. "Get me a Federation vehicle immediately and get one of our security people to the hospital as soon as possible. Kinsley wouldn't be attacked for no reason. Protect him,"

"Of course. The Federation Protects,"

"The Federation Protects," Bettie said.

Bettie just held both her little angels' hands as she looked at Sean and Harry. She couldn't believe that something so bad had happened to such a nice wonderful man and poor Graham was going to be heartbroken when he found out.

Bettie shook her head. She needed to focus because someone had just attacked one of her friends and she knew this was going to be a major, major incident. Especially because if she had learnt anything over the years it was that whatever was happening to her and her friends were always connected.

Kinsley's attack happened just a day before Graham's final day of his hearing.

The two had to be linked, Bettie had no idea how but the idea of the connection excited her a lot more than she ever wanted to admit.

CHAPTER 2
10th November 2023
Maidstone, England

Of all the damn places Detective Graham Adams didn't want to be, Maidstone Kent Police headquarters had to be on top of the list. He sat on a very uncomfortable blue fabric chair in a large white room with a huge floor-to-ceiling window to his left, but the views were hardly great.

He didn't want to see all the traffic, concrete buildings and shops of Maidstone. He wanted to see his girlfriend, his children and his nephews. He didn't want to be in a silly kangaroo court that was designed simply by people that didn't like him.

All Graham wanted to be doing was out solving crimes, helping people and just doing what he did best which was serving and protecting the innocent people of Kent. He loved his job and he wasn't going to allow corrupt cops or idiots to railroad him.

Graham leant on the small plastic desk like the

horrible things he used to draw on back in secondary school to annoy his teachers. And he just stared at the three Panel members as they sat behind a long row of desks with files, papers and laptops on it.

The bitter, sweet aromas of strong black coffee, sticky glazed doughnuts and burnt bacon sandwiches filled the air and Graham licked his lips as the taste of bacon cruelly formed on his tongue. The smell had to be coming from the bullpen just outside the room but the silver blinds were pulled so Graham couldn't see who it was.

Or why they were being mean by torturing him with such sensational and tasty smells.

The chairwoman coughed.

He had never liked the chair of the misconduct hearing, Superintended Gabriella Martin, or just Gabby to everyone in the police because her name was too hard to spell. She might have been a good cop but Graham could tell that her uniform had been ironed and flattened to an inch of its life and she was trying to impress someone that wasn't there.

Graham had never met the independent member of the panel, a member of the public was the member of the panel meant to be represent the public interest with their own non-policing and experiences.

It had been two days so far and Graham still didn't know the man's name but he didn't like his blue shirt, chequered red trousers and tan shoes. He looked like a dick and Graham needed to make sure these people found him innocent.

Then the last member of the panel wasn't here yet, but Graham couldn't complain too much. His representative from the union wasn't here yet either.

It was annoying as hell but Graham had to admit the man was next to useless and considering he was facing three made-up Gross Misconduct charges, he really wanted someone good sitting next to him.

"Mr Adams," Gabby said, "we will start in a few minutes because Richard is coming up now. Your union man is unable and whilst it is your right to request a new representative, I think we can both agree that you might be better off without one,"

Graham couldn't believe how dark, evil and condescending the woman's voice was. He completely agreed with her about his representative, he *should* have had one but he liked to believe he was good enough at proving he was innocent to not need one.

And they were useless anyway.

"I agree," Graham said.

"Good morning all," Richard said as he came in wearing his normal Sergeant uniform.

Graham hated wearing his police uniform. He was more than glad it wasn't too small for him but the uniform just felt so alien to him like the uniform didn't actually show who he was anymore. Something Graham really didn't want to be the case but if he failed then he knew he was going to be out of the police for good.

"Mr Adams for the past two days we have read submissions and testimonies from your fellow officers regarding your conduct and we have had three witnesses talk to the hearing about such matters," Gabby said.

Graham forced himself not to roll his eyes. He had no idea how hearing the testimonies of former cops that had been struck off the force because Graham had proved they were corrupt and abusing their powers, were worth anything.

And the rest of the testimonies were from cops that Graham knew were corrupt but couldn't prove. Or from such spineless men that Graham wondered what threat they had received to make them spread their lies in the hearing.

"Quite frank Mr Adams," Richard said, "unless you have any convincing evidence to prove that the Gross Misconduct charges did not occur then I suggest we go to deliberations and next steps regarding your future in the police,"

"Remind me of the charges," Graham said hoping it would give him a little more time so he could think of something useful.

"A police officer should always be responsible and embody the police conduct of Confidentiality," Gabby said. "Yet you have time and time again shared confidential information with the British Private Eye Federation without approval of your superior officer,"

Graham couldn't exactly deny that but it was only when the police were being stupid and it was UK law that the Federation had access to anything the police did.

"Also," Richard said, "a police officer must show respect and integrity towards higher ranking officers and follow their orders. You never have,"

Graham didn't have the heart to point out that he had always followed the orders and instructions of his bosses, sometimes even when the orders where silly, but he had always disregarded dangerous and silly orders that would allow killers and criminals to get away with their crimes.

"And finally," the independent man said, "there is evidence that you have not embodied the police ideals about diversity and equality,"

Graham laughed. He couldn't help it. It was him that always exposed and challenged and punished sexist, racist and homophobic officers.

"That's funny?" Gabby asked.

"It is a lie and just call in Detective Kinsley to support me here," Graham said.

The three members of the panel looked at each other.

Gabby leant forward and gave Graham an evil grin. "Mr Adams, Detective Kinsley was under police investigation himself last night for similar Gross Misconduct charges like yourself but he was attacked and currently lies in a coma,"

Graham just leant backwards. This couldn't be happening. Kinsley was such a great man who truly believed in the power, good and duty of the police (something Graham hadn't believed in for months) and there was no way Kinsley would ever break a rule.

So Graham had no idea what the hell was going on but something was happening in the police and that scared Graham to his very core.

CHAPTER 3
10th November 2023
Canterbury, England

Bettie definitely knew it was approaching winter as she walked up the long sterile grey-white corridor of Canterbury Hospital. There were red strips of plastic near the bottom of the grey walls and the tops near the ceiling, Bettie had no idea what colour-coding system the hospital used, but she didn't care.

She just kept walking up the long corridor towards where the Matron had told her where Kinsley was. The dear Matron had no idea why Bettie wanted to see him, and she had no idea herself, but a few thousand pounds worth of donations towards the new children's ward silent her a lot quicker than Bettie would have liked.

At least the innocent sick children could benefit from the attack.

There were plenty of large grey metal fire doors shooting off the corridor and Bettie nodded to male and female nurses as they walked about frowning and trying to fight a battle they would lose, in their tight blue uniforms.

Bettie knew most of them were working 13 hours shifts because the NHS was so stretched, underfunded and a sheer nightmare. As much as Bettie knew her monthly donations of hundreds of thousands of pounds to all the NHS trusts in Kent helped, she knew it was never ever enough.

And her extra money was a mere drop in the ocean compared to what the NHS actually needed.

Bettie shook the idea away that wasn't her problem for now, she had to focus on Kinsley and stopping the monsters that dared to hurt him.

The choking smells of bleach, oranges and sickness filled the air as Bettie went along the corridor. Judging by the cleaning crew and a large group of sad looking male nurses, Bettie guessed that a patient had died here recently.

Something she was determined not to let happen to Kinsley.

Bettie smiled as a very tall, muscular and scary looking man stepped out of the hospital room at the very edge of the corridor. It was great to see Fran had contacted the best of the best for this protection detail.

Bettie had met former SAS Commander Neil Slater a few months ago when she was interviewing for a personal security detail after her assassination attempt. She didn't end up hiring anyone because she was only doing it to keep her membership and Graham happy.

But Neil with his massive biceps, sapphire eyes and incredible smile wasn't exactly the sort of man anyone would forget. As much as Bettie would have wanted Harry and Sean with her, they were looking after the kids back at home.

Bettie just smiled as the kids were going to have an amazing day.

"Madame President," Neil said bowing his head slightly, "the target is secured and I am monitoring the situation at both ends of the corridor and I have personally vetted the hospital staff on this ward and in the kitchen areas,"

Bettie smiled because she had actually forgotten just how effective Neil was at his job.

"Thank you Commander. What have you heard from the nurses and paramedics?" Bettie asked as she went into the hospital room.

As Neil started talking about how he had gotten the information, Bettie was impressed by the hospital room. It was large, airy with grey walls, a single wooden chair and table in the far corner and the hospital bed was made from icy cold metal and its greyness almost matched Kinsley's complexion.

Bettie went over to her friend and shook her head. She took his hand, that was connected to thousands of little machines, in hers and she couldn't believe this had happened.

Kinsley had a massive tube down his throat, he

didn't have a hospital gown on and his bedsheets barely covered his waist and legs. All sorts of medical devices were connected to his chest and Bettie knew, just knew he was in a very bad shape.

But Bettie was surprised that all the bruises, slices and cuts were to his stomach, chest and probably his legs. Bettie looked at his arms and they were all shades of black, blue and purple but there were barely any wounds to his head.

These attackers didn't want to kill him, and Bettie seriously couldn't understand that.

"Has anyone tried to visit?" Bettie asked.

Neil smiled at her and Bettie realised that he had been telling her stuff but she hadn't been listening.

"Was he a friend?" Neil asked not daring to leave the doorway in case of an attack.

"Yes," Bettie said, "he was a good friend of Graham's, a great man with Harrison and Elizabeth, and I think occasional fuck buddy for Harry and Sean before he met his boyfriend,"

Neil grinned, Bettie didn't deny that they were all close with Kinsley in different ways but this was so hard.

"I know he is in good care here Miss English," Neil said knowing how tough this must be for her. "And the doctors say the damage isn't as bad as it looks,"

Bettie was glad to hear it but she so badly wanted a lead to help her catch the bastard.

"The doctors did leave his personal effects," Neil

said knowing that might give Bettie a lead, "and I noticed there were a few interesting things,"

Bettie went over to the small wooden table and it was only now she realised that the personal effects were there in a small plastic bag.

Neil stood up perfectly straight. "An Inspector calls,"

Bettie frowned at him. "What?"

"Inspector Granger's coming up the corridor now," Neil said. "Do I let him through?"

Bettie took out her phone and started taking pictures she didn't want to touch anything just in case there were criminal fingerprints on them and she didn't have time to process the evidence through the Federation.

"Stall," Bettie said.

Bettie noticed a small memory stick so as much as she didn't want to do it she opened the bag and when to reach into it.

"Step aside or I will arrest you!" someone shouted.

Bettie didn't get a damn chance to grab it. She had to protect Neil otherwise Kinsley would be open to an attack.

"Let him through," Bettie said.

And she just knew that things were about to get a lot worse.

Little did Bettie know just how bad things were about to get.

CHAPTER 4
10th November 2023
Maidstone, England

Graham flat out couldn't believe that something had happened to poor Kinsley, they had only had lunch together a few days ago. He seemed so happy to be working on cases, he was having a great time with his boyfriend and he just couldn't be happier with life.

If Graham had been an active detective, he fully intended to storm out of this damn kangaroo court and find the bastards that did this to his friend, and a fine police detective. But if he knew his wonderful girlfriend as much as he liked to think he did, then Bettie was already investigating.

He had to trust her, which wasn't hard at all.

Graham just looked at the three awful faces of the panel members, and he could have sworn they were smiling at him. Maybe they enjoyed watching his pain, maybe they knew exactly what happened or maybe they had a role to play in the attack.

Graham couldn't prove it but the timing was a lot weirder than he would have liked. It was one thing for him to experience this whole kangaroo court but for someone to attack a dear friend of his at the same time, it was too much of a coincidence.

And Graham hated those.

"Mr Adams," Gabby said, "if you are quite done with your feelings about Detective Kinsley we must move on,"

Graham sat up perfectly straight. "Actually Gov, I would like to ask some questions please about the incident and the events leading up to it,"

Gabby shook her head. "Impossible. This is a Misconduct Hearing against you and you are no longer a detective,"

"I disagree," the independent man said.

"Seriously Oliver," Gabby said.

At least Graham finally knew the man's name and he might even have a potential friend in this damn hearing.

"It is the job of this panel to review Mr Adams' conduct in relation to the charges," Oliver said, "and your own rules state that this Panel is as much an inquisitorial example of the justice system as adversarial,"

Graham was surprised this layperson knew that much about police rules and regulations. He had almost forgotten that the panel could do whatever it wanted, called in whoever it wanted and ask whatever questions it wanted (the inquisitorial justice system) but Graham also had the right to use his own argument to combat against the panels' narrative of events.

Graham knew research might have shown the Inquisitorial system was better at getting to the truth but that relied on the panel members being relatively unbiased, something Graham felt wasn't what was happening here.

"Gov," Graham said, "and I kindly request to use what is happening to Detective Kinsley as evidence that I care about my fellow officers, something that was apparently discredited in some testimony yesterday,"

Gabby tapped her pen on the desk a few times and she nodded. "I will allow a fixed number of questions to allow Mr Adams to proof himself then we can continue with *our* discussions and line of enquiries,"

Graham hated that that was all he was going to get but he had to make this count.

"I will be honest that I am friends with Detective Kinsley and it is because of that I fail to see why he would be under investigation. He is one of the greatest cops I have ever met,"

Gabby looked at the other two and they both nodded to her.

"Detective Kinsley was formally suspended as of end of shift yesterday pending a formal inquiry into his illegal activity. The charge is he was illegally investigating fellow officers,"

Graham nodded. That would make sense, Kinsley was one of the best cops he knew and if Kinsley suspected a cop or two or more were dirty then he would have investigated it.

It was a badly kept secret in policing that the Police Watchdog was extremely useful but it was next to useless unless you went *through* your superiors to get an appointment or to give the suspicions a little more weight.

Clearly Kinsley believed he couldn't do that.

"How is the investigation into the attack going?" Graham asked.

Gabby shrugged. "I know CID is investigating but they have yet to yield anything useful and the department is currently snowed under in Canterbury and the Superintendent has not granted permission for officers from other divisions to help out,"

"Why haven't *you?*" Graham asked knowing that Gabby would be the superintendent in charge of most of the Kent area including Maidstone and Canterbury.

She smiled. "And that is the end of your questions. I think we can conclude from that set of questions you might be concerned about your fellow officers but your questions and actions raise more questions than answers,"

Graham really hated her.

Richard nodded and started writing things down. "Like why did Mr Adams not ask about the welfare of his fellow officer? Why did he imply a superintendent is not doing her job properly? Another example of his inability to respect the police hierarchy. And why did Mr Adams not use his questions to defend himself better?"

Graham so badly wanted to tell him it was because Gabby had cut his questions short. Normally he would have left it but he was annoyed so he just wanted to ask one more question.

"Who was Kinsley investigating?" Graham asked.

The three panel members shrugged but Graham could see Gabby was smiling. He could have guessed that Kinsley was investigating her but if that was true, Graham had to believe Kinsley that she was a dirty officer trying to derail him and his career.

And Graham had no idea how to stop her when she was in charge of the panel that would ultimately decide his fate.

He really hoped Bettie was making a lot more progress than him.

UNIFORMED CABAL

CHAPTER 5
10th November 2023
Canterbury, England

Bettie just backed away from the personal effects sitting on the small wooden table in Kinsley's hotel room as Inspector Granger walked in and grabbed them like they belonged to him.

Inspector Granger was a new one to Bettie and she didn't really know what to make of him. He was a large middle-aged man with a balding head and a slight beard. Bettie wasn't sure if he would ever win any beauty rewards judging by the massive black shopping bags under his eyes but he focused on him for a moment.

She couldn't tell if he was smiling or frowning or even both.

Bettie got the sense that Granger was a cold man and the deep frown line carved into his stony face didn't exactly do much to convince her otherwise. She might not have been officially hired to investigate the attack but she wanted to.

She had to do it for Kinsley, and chances are him or his boyfriend would pay her for her investigation services anyway later on.

"It's a damn shame," Granger said.

Bettie looked at Neil who was standing by the door looking ready to strike at any moment.

"It is. He was a good man," Bettie said.

Granger laughed. "Then you didn't know him very well. He was outspoken, always critical of us real cops and he was a pain. No cop deserves this and I didn't want the Hearing but my Superintendent forced my hand,"

Bettie forced herself not to frown or spit at this man. She had been dating Graham and investigating crime for far too many years helping vulnerable groups to know exactly what *real* cops meant.

Inspector Granger was a foul sexist, racist, homophobe of a cop but she couldn't understand why he cared about Kinsley then. And what was that about a Hearing?

"You're Graham's girlfriend, right?"

Bettie extended her hand. "Bettie English, private eye and President of the Federation,"

Granger looked down at her hand and looked at it and backed away like it was diseased or something.

"What was this about a Hearing?" Bettie asked.

"Your friend Kinsley is under investigation for the exact same charges as your boyfriend. We need to stop calling him Detective Kinsley because he was suspended after all,"

Bettie nodded and gave him a weak smile. She didn't want to make a complete enemy of him just yet but clearly something larger was happening here. And Bettie had read through transcripts of tons of Misconduct Hearings over recent months and absolutely no cop got done for the *exact* same charges.

But Inspector Granger didn't give Bettie the impression that he was the type of man to mix up his words.

Both Graham and Kinsley were being investigated for *exact* charges. Something that should be impossible.

"Maybe we can investigate this together," Bettie said. "I know the police are stretched and the Federation-"

"Is a group of pointless amateur detectives that don't know when to stop. Investigating crime is a job for the trained police, not a bunch of amateurs,"

"Do you realise we have a Royal Charter, university-level training requirements and are legally allowed to operate by permission of the UK Government?" Bettie asked.

"And so are so many other pointless groups," Granger said. "I am in charge of the investigation and if you dare to interfere then I will arrest you and every single private eye you throw in my way,"

Bettie forced herself not to throw her arms up in the air because she had lost the personal effects, lost her chance to work *with* the police and now the lead investigator was threatening to arrest her.

Things really couldn't get much worse.

Bettie shook her head as Granger walked away and then a young male nurse walked in looking rather sheepish and just frozen as he looked at Kinsley.

"I thought it was a mistake," the nurse said, his hands shaking.

Bettie went over to him. "Did you know him?"

"He was a neighbour and he was four years old than me and when I came out to my parents, they took it badly, kicked me out but Kinsley gave me safe until my parents had realised I was the same kid they had always loved,"

Bettie had always liked Kinsley for how kind and amazing and brilliant he was.

"We stayed in touch and met up once a month for drinks and a catch-up," the nurse said. "It's a shame what happened. I hope you catch the bastard,"

The nurse went to walk away but Bettie placed a gentle hand on his arm. "Actually is there anything mentioned by the nurses not in the medical evidence?"

The nurse nodded. "A police officer phoned us as soon as Kinsley entered the official hospital database. It was weird. Crazy weird like, you know, they were already in the hospital database,"

Bettie didn't dare react in case it stopped him talking.

"I was the one that answered the phone and he

ordered me to make sure no one got a hold of the memory stick until the police officer in charge of the investigation turned up,"

"Jason!" a woman shouted, probably the Matron.

"Thank you," Bettie said.

"Catch the bastard," the nurse said as he left.

Bettie went over to Kinsley's hospital bed and leant on it, looking at her injured friend.

"What were you investigating?" she asked.

"That's weird about the memory stick," Neil said.

"Agreed. I need my team on this and the Federation is involved now whether Granger wants it or not," Bettie said turning to face Neil. "Protect him please and keep him alive. I don't know what's happening but something is. And if people are willing to attack a detective on a well-lit street I doubt a hospital will be a challenge to their courage,"

"Of course Madame President. The Federation Protects,"

Bettie laughed as she said the saying back to him and she left.

She just had a feeling that she was going to need all the protection she could get if her theory about dodgy police officers was true.

CHAPTER 6
10th November 2023
Maidstone, England

Graham nodded his thanks to the young police constable as she passed him a very lukewarm mug of coffee and did the same to the members of the panel. He enjoyed the small amount of warmth it allowed him but he really wanted to be out there investigating what happened to his friend.

That wasn't happening until he was free of this panel so he had to prove this was a kangaroo court and that he was innocent.

"Let us discuss the matter of so-called confidentiality," Graham said.

Gabby smiled, shook her head and leant forward. "Mr Adams, over the past two days we have heard over fifty incidences where you have shared information about people, police activities and suspects under police investigation with the Federation owned by your wife,"

"She isn't my wife,"

Gabby sneered. "That is wrong. I would have thought you would have more morals about not having kids out of wedlock and seriously detective, you would trust a woman you aren't married to with this sort of police information,"

Graham didn't dare react. It would have been okay or bearable if she was joking or just trying to goat him into a reaction that would make her case easier. But he knew she wasn't because Gabby had always had a reputation for being slightly sexist herself and thinking that men were the only qualified people to do important jobs.

It was actually rumoured to be the reason why she had turned down the Chief Constable job two years ago.

Graham was rather glad she had now.

"Bettie English," Graham said, "is a strong, trustworthy woman that is the chief of discretion. Just ask any of her clients,"

Richard shook his head. "You know that isn't true because of the testimony we heard yesterday,"

"Testimony based on lies," Graham said and regretted saying it as soon as it left his mouth.

Gabby laughed. "This is what we mean Mr Adams, you have no respect for your fellow officers and the hierarchy, rules and regulations of this police force,"

He couldn't believe this was actually happening. As soon as he started to dig himself out of one mess, he sunk in deeper into another mess.

This was a nightmare.

"You do realise," Graham said, "that I have the highest closure and solve rate in Kent Police. My cases never fail to get a conviction because I always get air-tight evidence and I am well-respected in the community,"

"Now who is lying?" Gabby asked. "There isn't a single police officer that respects you,"

Graham stood up and frowned. "I wasn't talking about the police community. I was talking about the community of the public that I took an oath to serve and protect when I joined the police over a decade ago,"

Gabby stood up too. "Sit down Mr Adams,"

"No," Graham said surprised at the icy coldness in his voice. "I will not because if you really want to get rid of me, a damn good cop that loves solving crimes, protecting victims and helping innocent people through high-quality work. Then I do not know what the police stands for anymore,"

Gabby shook her head.

"And yes, this Misconduct Hearing is a kangaroo court designed to discredit me. I do not know why but I know someone is pulling the strings of this panel,"

Oliver shook his head. "Mr Adams, I have to agree with my peers here. You and your conspiracy theories do make you unfit to be a police officer so I am agreeing with them that we need to talk and recommend your dismissal,"

Graham's hands formed fists. "If you do that then you will lose a police officer that loves his job, but also always stands up to sexist, racism and homophobia. Something so few in this police force does,"

Gabby shook her head. "Something you keep saying but you fail to notice all the-"

Graham waved her silent. "I know exactly what the Top-brass plan to do about these problems. Nothing. You come out with all your procedures, all your ideas and all your policies that make you look good to the general public. But I know the truth and I have worked in this police culture for over a decade,"

"Get out," Gabby said.

Graham shook his head and walked away. "You can text me your decision because I have real investigative work to do,"

"You aren't a cop anymore Graham," Richard said. "Don't do anything you'll regret,"

Graham smiled. "I might still be suspended but by God are there other ways to make a difference in the world and that all starts with the Federation,"

As he started walking down the long corridor outside, he took out his phone and called the woman he loved.

They needed a game plan now because something major was happening and he had no idea where to start.

CHAPTER 7
10th November 2023
Canterbury, England

Bettie had no idea at all when her living room with its wonderful white walls, landscape paintings and large black sofas had become the unofficial war room of the Federation but she was more than happy that it had.

She was sitting on a very large black sofa with a small mug of chai latte in her hands, she loved its sweet, creamy spiciness that warmed her through on the coldest of days. She watched and smiled as Harrison and Elizabeth played on the floor with Harry Sean and thankfully everyone else was here too.

She wrapped her arms around Graham's fit sexy body as he sat down next to her with a glass of cold orange squash, she couldn't believe what had happened at the damn hearing, but she was certain now that something was going on.

She didn't know what but she was determined to

find out what.

Her assistant Fran sat on another black sofa wearing black jeans, a white blouse and ten-inch heels that Bettie was fairly sure would kill her if she ever wore them.

And her best friend in the entire world Senior Forensic Specialist Zoey Quill was on her laptop as she was working at the moment. She was in charge of all the forensic teams and testing for Kent Police so she didn't really want to take up too much of her time.

"Thanks for coming everyone," Bettie said.

"If someone attacks Kinsley they attack us all," Sean said.

Bettie was really starting to realise her team, herself and the Federation were basically the NATO of the private eye world. She just smiled at that realisation, that was funny.

"Zoey," Bettie said, "anything on the forensics yet,"

"Come one Bet," she said, "it was an assault on a police officer but it wasn't murder. I have murder cases to run tests on so I cannot jump the queue and Inspector Granger has made me promise not to give the Federation any evidence from this case,"

"Damn," Bettie said nodding at Fran so she would know to look him up.

"I'm not even meant to be talking to you," Zoey said.

"Anything from your highly trained eye,"

Graham said, "and beautiful eyes,"

Bettie gently elbowed him in the ribs knowing that he was joking, or at least hoping so.

"Crowbar or something like that shape," Zoey said. "Best I can come up and Mr asshole has entered the building. If I get something I'll call,"

Bettie nodded her thanks as Zoey ended the call and she looked at Fran hoping she had something.

"Need a moment longer," Fran said.

Bettie slipped down on the floor and grabbed one of Elizabeth's bears to get her to come over to her.

Graham took a sip of his drink. "Granger doesn't work in East or North Kent. He's more a west Kent sort of guy so I have no clue why he's working this one,"

Bettie tickled Elizabeth as she came over and fell on the floor laughing and screaming in happiness.

"Inspector Thomas Granger," Fran said, "nothing that jumps out. No financial problems, no criminal records and nothing else that exciting,"

"Why would a cop have a criminal record?" Harry asked before gasping a moment later realising just how beyond stupid that question was.

"What was the last count?" Bettie asked.

Graham shrugged. "Maybe five hundred out of tens of thousands of police officers do have criminal records,"

Bettie just couldn't believe that. That was bad and it was a shame.

"No wife," Fran said. "No girlfriend or anything that exciting and yeah, Inspector Granger has such a boring life,"

"It was worth a shot," Bettie said smiling at Elizabeth as her daughter tapped her on the arm.

"Why was Kinsley coming here?" Sean asked running a hand through his pink highlighted hair.

"I get the sense that he was investigating Superintendent Gabby for some reason and others," Graham said. "I suspect if what you say was true then he had a memory stick or something that he wanted to give us,"

Bettie couldn't disagree. Everything seemed to be connected to the damn memory stick and if Kinsley was coming to her last night to give her the information then she needed that memory stick.

Bettie's phone buzzed from a blocked number and as much as she wanted to decline it, she answered it.

"Miss English," a man said, "I am sorry to call you out the blue but I wanted to check on my boyfriend and he left me a voicemail,"

Bettie clicked her fingers and put it on speaker.

"You're on speaker and Kinsley is alive for now," Bettie said.

There was a very loud sigh of relief on the other side of the line.

"I'm on assignment at the moment in the middle east and only returned to France this morning to cover the protests. I'm Oscar Peterson, Kinsley's boyfriend,"

"What did the message say?" Sean asked.

"Hi Sean," Oscar said like they knew each other. "Kinsley mentioned how he had the proof on the Cabal, he knows the 5 members and he was coming to you to bring the evidence,"

Bettie was relieved to finally have confirmation that something was going on, but the very idea of there being a Cabal in the police made up of five people actually scared her.

"Thank you for this," Bettie said.

"Get the-"

Bettie covered the speaker part of the phone as Oscar said the *c-word*.

"We will. I promise and I have him protected,"

Bettie cut the line and Graham kissed her on the head.

"Can you keep that promise?" Graham asked.

Bettie grinned. "Of course I can because you're going to break into Kent Police and get that memory stick for us,"

CHAPTER 8
10th November 2023
Canterbury, England

An hour later, Graham had to admit that as much as he loved Bettie, he couldn't deny that she had lost her mind with this crazy idea. Because it was simply impossible for someone to break into a police station and extract evidence for an attack on a police officer.

It simply couldn't happen.

So Graham hugged Bettie tight as she finally agreed that the plan wouldn't work and he finished off his third glass of squash and they set about thinking about their next move.

Graham still didn't want to know that there was a group of five people in the police that were influencing the running of the police force and all the other illegal things that Cabals did to make sure they controlled things behind the scenes.

But it would explain a hell of a lot including why

he had been summoned to a Misconduct Hearing in the first place.

Graham slid down on the floor next to Harrison and helped him build a tower of blocks that he promptly smashed over.

Graham rebuilt it for him.

"What do we have on Gabby?" Bettie asked.

"She's a dick," Graham said smiling as Harrison smashed down the blocks again. "She has to be involved and I get the sense that Kinsley was investigating her,"

"Impossible," Fran said, "because I *may* have hacked Kinsley's emails and she was helping him,"

"What do you mean?" Graham asked rebuilding the tower one last time for Harrison before everyone went over to Fran to look at her laptop.

"Look," Fran said bringing up emails between Gabby and Kinsley.

Graham couldn't believe this. He was sure that Gabby was involved but all these emails showed that she was helping him, making sure he was okay and she was constantly telling him to be careful.

And the tone was almost intimate on her end like she wanted Kinsley but she couldn't for obvious reasons.

"That's one thing to look at," Bettie said. "We need to talk to her. You and me can do that later,"

Graham nodded. He always loved spending time with Bettie whatever they were doing and if he was talking to Gabby then he was going to need moral support.

"Look at the hearing panel," Graham said. "Look at Richard and Oliver,"

Fran nodded as her fingers danced over the keyboard. "Oliver is a Director of Human Resources at a small local law firm. He applied to be the independent member of police conduct panel two years ago,"

Graham didn't know why her voice was getting higher.

"Because his father was dismissed as a police officer at that time and there was a major rumour at the time that it was a kangaroo court designed to get rid of him,"

Graham noticed Bettie, Sean and Harry were looking at each other.

"Daddy what's protest?" Elizabeth asked.

Clearly something had happened earlier that he didn't know about so he quickly told Elizabeth what a protest was and she nodded and went off playing.

"That protest earlier by Lott's café," Bettie said. "Harry you said that was about a police officer being dismissed. Do you know who?"

He nodded and bought up a news article on his phone. Graham actually knew the police officer and he had no idea the cop had been dismissed, Officer Derrick Foog was a good man and very respectful. He was always helping black officers into the profession.

"Racism was the reason given for the Hearing," Fran said.

"Something Derrick really wasn't," Graham said.

"That's another lead we need to follow up. We'll talk to the wife or whoever was protesting earlier," Bettie said.

"And I want to talk to Inspector Granger," Graham said not realising until now that was what he wanted to do.

"Why?" Sean asked.

"Because I want to get him to stop being so anal about all of this. We need that memory stick and maybe if it comes to me he might open up,"

"Daddy not cop," Harrison said.

Bettie laughed and hugged him. Graham both loved and hated the honesty of children at times.

Graham picked Harrison up and hugged him. "Well Daddy might still be able to get through to him,"

Harrison kissed Graham and waved his arms about pointing to the tower of blocks.

He knew there was a lot to investigate and it annoyed him a lot more than he wanted to admit that they had a lot of leads but they still didn't have a clue about who could be in charge of this cabal and what their end goal actually was.

Something that really concerned Graham.

CHAPTER 9
10th November 2023
Maidstone, England

As much as Bettie had wanted beautiful, sexy Graham to come with her to talk to Gabby, she had understood why he had wanted to talk to Granger instead. It still made her smile at the excellent point little Harrison had made about Graham's talking cop-to-cop theory was about as dead as Kinsley almost was.

But she loved him and his determination anyway.

Bettie pulled her thick black trench coat tightly around her as she waited in the middle of the large Kent Police car park as she leant on a red Ford Fiesta belonging to Gabby.

The car park was largely empty of people but it was filled to the brim with black, blue and red hatchbacks of various makes and models. It was a rather depressing reflection of the awful pay that police officers had these days but with there being no people about, Bettie was hardly concerned about people watching and judging Gabby for talking to her.

An icy cold wind blew through the car park and howled as it went against the large concrete and brick buildings at the very edges of the car park. They were all police buildings with a few floors rented out to businesses as the police tried to plug immense holes in their budgets.

Bettie smiled as a very grumpy-looking Gabby in her police (and very cold) police uniform walked towards her.

"I should get you done for harassment," Gabby said feeling how cold her uniform was. "I know you're Graham's girlfriend and the panel has already made its recommendation,"

"Then you know full-well that he isn't a cop anymore," Bettie said.

Gabby took out her car keys. "Of course I am aware of that. I watched the Chief Constable sign off Graham's retirement papers immediately. He is not a problem for Kent Police to concern itself with,"

Bettie leant more on her car.

"Is there a point to your visit or are you always a dick?" Gabby said shivering.

"That depends on who you ask. I know you were helping Kinsley investigate corrupt officers within the heart of Kent Police,"

Bettie loved it how Gabby sniffed, looked around and stood up perfectly straight almost as if she was trying to look scary. But Bettie forced herself not to laugh, Gabby was so tiny she would be the last person Bettie found scary.

"How did you know?"

"I have my methods Superintendent so why don't you tell me what happened? I think we both know the longer we stand out here the higher the chance of someone seeing us together. And reporting to whoever the corrupt cops are and you might end up like Kinsley,"

Gabby frowned and Bettie noticed her hands were shaking so much the car keys were jiggling together.

Gabby unlocked the car and suggested Bettie inside.

Bettie was surprised by how fresh and nice the inside of the car was. It still had that wonderful new car smell and it was spotless, she had no idea when her own car had been this clean.

Definitely before she had had kids.

Gabby got in the other side and frowned. "I helped Kinsley because he was hot that was it,"

Bettie shook her head. "He was gay, had a loving boyfriend and there was no chance you could be together. Surely?"

Gabby smiled. "Of course not but he was a good friend. I'm recently divorced and my husband has everything. He lied in court saying that my police job kept me too busy to raise our kids, and there's something in my past from twenty years ago that he played up. My husband has the house, the kids and everything,"

Bettie wanted to feel sorry for her but if there was even a small chance she had hurt Kinsley then Bettie wanted her nailed to the wall forever.

"Kinsley helped me through the divorce, he was helping me explore options to get my kids back and, yeah he was a good man. And I was stupid enough to fall for him along the way,"

Bettie felt a little sorry for her. She just couldn't imagine not being able to see Harrison and Elizabeth, that would have killed her completely.

"The Cabal?" Bettie asked.

Gabby looked around. "Three weeks ago Kinsley came to me asking about why several progressive policies by Kent Police that would have protected minorities and sexual assault victims better were abandoned, and why five Misconduct hearings were dismissed against three police officers known as *The Pinchers*,"

Bettie shook her head in disgust. She couldn't believe that a group of officers would actually be known for pinching and sexually harassing women and no one had done anything to nip it in the bud.

It was outrageous.

"I said to Kinsley I would look into it," Gabby said hating the whole situation, "and I found that it was simply a matter of a group of police officers in high ranking positions coordinating things and pulling strings,"

"What do you mean?" Bettie asked not really

understanding.

Gabby ducked a little as a police constable walked past. "I mean I found evidence of police emails between five people that never should have been emailing about these Progressive Policies. Police Policy is a job only for the Chief Constable and other high rank officials,"

Bettie nodded. That made sense.

"But the five emails I discovered where all from detectives,"

Bettie waved her hands about. "Are you telling me the five Cabal members are all Detectives? Not Chief Constables and other high ranking people?"

Gabby nodded. "And-"

Bullets screamed through the air.

Bettie grabbed Gabby.

Pulling her down.

Windows exploded.

Glass rained down on them.

Bettie's hand turned bloody.

It wasn't her blood.

The windscreen shattered.

Bettie screamed.

A bullet hit somewhere close to her.

Then it all stopped and Bettie didn't need to check Gabby to know she was dead.

And that meant these detectives were escalating their attacks.

CHAPTER 10
10th November 2023
Maidstone, England

Graham was absolutely bloody outraged when he got to the immense car park that was swarming with crime scene techs in their white canvas suits taking pictures, collecting shards of glass and more.

He had no idea how the hell this had happened. This was an assassination of a police Superintendent in board daylight, this was extreme even more for a secret Cabal.

Loud shouting, reporting of findings and more filled the icy cold air as detectives, inspectors and more constables than Graham knew the entire police force had running everywhere. Graham actually started to feel a little sick about what was happening, the beautiful woman he loved had almost been shot dead but he knew that never would have happened.

As much as Graham hated to admit it, this cabal was far too careful for Bettie to be dead. He believed that the cabal hadn't killed Kinsley because assaulting a cop meant a lot less resources were dedicated to an investigation compared to murder.

They were careful not to kill Kinsley but now the cabal felt the need to kill Gabby. Graham just didn't know why and he needed to see Bettie as soon as possible as she had been taken to the hospital at Fran's insistence.

Graham saw Granger standing with his arms folded standing next to two large white canvas tents belonging to the crime scene techs. Hopefully Granger might be more willing to talk now.

Graham went over to him.

"Inspector Granger," Graham said.

Granger clicked his fingers at two constables who were just gossiping about the weather from what Graham overheard.

"Take this civilian off my crime scene," Granger said.

Graham went to take out his badge but he hadn't had it for weeks now because of this damn kangaroo court.

"I trust you do not want to know what I do about this crime," Graham said hoping that might get Granger to listen to him.

Granger smiled. "Mr Adams, you are not a cop anymore. I do not care about your wild theories and it is officers like you that discredit the rest of us,"

Graham frowned.

"Do you realise Mr Adams," Granger said, "that

everything the news shows how a cop went rogue, every time a cop interferes with a woman and attacks them walking home, and every time a cop kills a minority just because they're racist. It makes life ten times harder for the rest of us,"

Graham nodded. "I know 99.9% of the cops in this police force are amazing. I will never forget that and that is why I promise you, I am being setup,"

Granger waved him away.

Graham went forward but the two constables grabbed him. Graham almost smiled as the grips were so weak he easily could have pushed himself out of their grips.

"What will it take for you to listen to me?" Graham asked. "There's a Cabal of police officers at play here and they beat Kinsley,"

Granger turned around and waved the two constables away and gestured Graham to walk with him.

He noticed that Granger was leading him towards the yellow police tape but Graham was just grateful for the chance to speak with him.

"You know about the Cabal?"

Graham nodded. He didn't want to say too much if Granger was involved.

"I have heard of things grew the grape vine but this is an internal police matter. I have control of the scene. I have the physical evidence and you have nothing,"

"I have the Federation," Graham said stopping in

his tracks.

Granger laughed. "The Federation is an interfering little organisation that has no real power in the world. Let the police investigate crime and just go home. You are not a cop and you never will be again. I will make sure of it,"

Graham watched as Granger clicked his fingers again to get the two constables back over but Graham shook his head and simply walked the three blocks to where he had parked his car outside a Chinese takeaway restaurant on the high street.

It was relatively empty probably because of the icy cold breeze and Graham was about to drive home when his phone rang.

It was Zoey Quill.

"Hi my dear," Graham said hoping that joke would cheer him up.

"You on pain killers or something,"

Graham laughed. "What you got for me?"

"Nothing good. I'll make my full report to Inspector Asshole later today but I recognise these bullets from a conference I attend three months ago. These are the exact same rounds as police-issued assault rifles used by tactical response,"

"Fuck," Graham said.

"Exactly this is very bad Graham," Zoey said hating how serious the situation was. "I'm telling you this because our girl was almost killed. How is she?"

Graham opened the driver's door. "I'm going to the hospital now but something isn't adding up. Why would a group of careful police officers suddenly decide to use police-issued weapons to kill Gabby?"

"Damn it. Inspector Asshole's coming. Find the bastards that almost killed my bestie,"

"Will do," Graham said hanging up.

As much as he wanted to believe there was an easy explanation for all of this, he knew things were always going to get a lot worse before they even started to get better.

Little did he realise just how bad things were going to get.

CHAPTER 11
10th November 2023
Canterbury, England

As Bettie leant on the nice, toasty warm bed end of Kinsley's hospital bed, she was surprised more than anything about how she was really affected by the shooting. She supposed part of it was because of the assassination attempts on her life a few months ago, but she was a little concerned.

She was more annoyed that Gabby had died. She seemed to be a good woman, a mother that loved her kids and Bettie just didn't get the sense that Gabby was a bad person.

They were back to square one without Gabby able to tell them more.

Fran sat in a small wooden chair on her laptop looking up some background information on Gabby and checking out some of the things that she had told Bettie before all hell broke loose.

Bettie was really glad that Graham was coming

soon and Sean and Harry were coming up as soon as they dropped the kids off at Bettie's mother's house.

Bettie looked at poor Kinsley. He looked so peaceful and his vitals looked a little better than earlier, but she still hated that this had happened to him. She absolutely had to get justice for him no matter the cost.

"I don't know what she meant," Fran said. "I have searched all of Gabby's official and unofficial police email accounts and I cannot find any mention of these five police detectives,"

"What about her personal accounts?" Bettie asked.

"That's what I mean too. There is no evidence she saw any emails, could she be lying?"

Bettie shook her head and went over to Kinsley's side and took a hand in hers. She so badly wished he was with them and he could tell them what he had found.

"We still that memory stick," Bettie said.

Fran laughed and passed Bettie her laptop and as Bettie read it, she was horrified to find that officially there was no memory stick entered in evidence. Inspector Granger had signed off on the evidence himself.

"The corrupt bastard," Bettie said. "I'll be talking again to him later on,"

Bettie couldn't believe what was happening here but she really didn't believe that Granger was the sort of man to be corrupt. He seemed to be upset about

Kinsley's attack to be involved and she had seen a glimpse of him as Fran forced her to go to the hospital.

He actually seemed like he wanted, truly wanted to know if she was okay after the constable took her statement.

"I know you did this earlier," Bettie said, "but does Granger have *anything* that could be used against him? Like blackmail material,"

Fran stood up and stood opposite her. "A daughter, twenty-one-year-old and she studies at university on a professional policing degree. There's a pending warning against her on the police systems for a drunk disorderly,"

Bettie shrugged. "Is that important?"

Fran took a drink from Kinsley's hospital cup. Bettie smiled and just couldn't believe her friend had done that.

"If anyone changed that pending to official. Maybe? I don't know enough about police hiring to know if it's important enough, but surely a clear record is better than nothing,"

"Screenshot that pending warning please in case someone does actually remove it from police records,"

Fran nodded and looked back down at her laptop and laughed.

Bettie grinned. "Someone's already done it?"

Fran simply nodded.

Bettie was rather glad that happened. It would

make sense for someone in a position of power to offer Granger a chance to get rid of it in exchange for him giving them the memory stick but that might be the Cabal's downfall.

Bettie took her own phone and was about to search up Granger's phone movements when Neil popped his head in.

"Graham's here," Neil said.

Bettie told Fran to look at where Granger had been today to see if there was a strange location that could have been where he met the Cabal to hand over the memory stick whilst she went out into the long grey corridor.

She hugged and kissed the man she loved and she was so glad to see him. Graham smelt so fresh, felt so warm and he was just perfect and amazing.

Bettie kissed his soft lips one more time and told him everything that Gabby had told her before she died.

"Five detectives, we can work with that," Graham said. "We still need to talk to the people protesting outside the café earlier but I think we are making progress,"

Bettie couldn't deny that but she felt like there was something she was missing and as much as she wanted to talk to Granger, she knew the protesters were most important for now. Especially considering how protesting was basically illegal in the UK these days so the sooner she spoke to them the sooner she might get answers.

Bettie was about to say something when Neil clicked his fingers.

"Madam President," he said, "I have a man and a woman downstairs at reception claiming to be police detectives and they want to see Kinsley,"

"Do you have a man or woman down there in reception?" Bettie asked.

Neil nodded and touched his ear. "Victoria, do not, I repeat do not allow those people up here."

A moment later Neil nodded and Bettie mockingly offered Graham her arm.

"Mr Adams shall we go and introduce ourselves to our guests?"

"I think we should Miss English,"

Bettie laughed as her and Graham stormed down the corridor to talk to these two detectives that were most certainly involved.

But first Bettie wanted to call Sean and Harry to get them to talk to the protesters because it just seemed like the world didn't want her talking to them with everything getting in her way.

And Bettie just couldn't understand why. What was so important the events of the day didn't want her talking to the protesters for?

UNIFORMED CABAL

CHAPTER 12
10th November 2023
Canterbury, England

Sean always loved helping his amazing auntie with whatever she needed for her investigations and it was even better when he got to do it with the sexy man he loved. Harry looked so fit and adorable in his black overcoat that highlighted just how fit he was.

They both went down the long cobblestone high street of Canterbury with the little (and large) red, green and black brick buildings lining each side. Tons of young university students like them went up and down the high street like a constantly churning river, and Sean really did love Canterbury. It was just such a warm, friendly city that was brilliant for people of all sexes, ages and sexualities.

Sean noticed a small group of police constables were standing across the high street from were three people protesting as they shouted, held up signs and Sean hated it as his stomach twisted.

They might have been on the opposite end of the high street to where their attack had happened but he still didn't like the look of police officers, despite Graham.

Sean felt Harry's hand tight as he felt his wonderful boyfriend start to slow down. Sean still couldn't forgive the police officers behind the attack for giving Harry brain damage that he was thankfully recovered from now, but the psychological fear and damage was still there.

"Kent Police is Corrupt Police!" a woman shouted.

Sean and Harry pushed their way through the small crowd of young university students which judging by their angry retorts they were professional policing students. Sean didn't have the heart to tell them that the police wasn't as perfect as their precious little textbooks would have them believe.

Sean appreciated that not every cop was bad but even the good ones turned a blind eye to the bad ones on most occasions.

"Excuse me," Sean said to a woman wearing a thick black coat, black jeans and had long blond hair. "I'm the nephew of Bettie English,"

Sean had been working with his auntie way too long for him not to know that her name was a powerful tool in getting people to talk to him. Yet he hadn't used it as a pickup line for now, if times ever went wrong with Harry he might have to try that out.

Sean laughed and shook the thought away.

"Mum," the woman shouted over to a middle-aged woman in a long black dress. "It's the Federation,"

A few moments later Sean nodded his thanks to the daughter as the older woman came over and Sean shook her very firm hand.

"What can I do for you Mr English?" the woman asked.

"Your protests might be connected to a Cabal we're investigating,"

The woman jumped up in the air. "Thank the Lord. Finally someone has pieced it together my husband was a damn good man and they derailed him and his career,"

"I'm sorry to hear that. Believe me I know the power of corrupt cops," Sean said gripping Harry's hand.

The woman looked at their hands and nodded. "I read the article last June, I'm sorry. What do you need from me?"

"Anything you can tell us about the people your husband suspected that would be a great start. And is there a chance we can talk to your husband, Derrick Foog please?"

The woman frowned. "Killed himself two weeks ago. He hung himself in his mancave I tried to help him honest. I hounded him to talk to me, I made him all the psych appointments I could but-"

Sean hugged her. She didn't need to explain herself to him, he knew the power of suicide all too well and how it seemed like a great way to end it all and stop the pain that swirled and twirled around inside a person.

But Sean also knew that sometimes there was just no helping some people like his best friends, but it sounded like Mrs Foog had done everything she could.

And the woman's weak smile looked like she understood that.

Sean looked at Harry to make sure he was okay but he was focusing on the police constables across the street. They were starting to walk over to the protesters and they had their batons out.

It was pathetic how protesting was basically illegal now in the UK and even if the police thought a protest *might* get disruptive the protesters could be legally arrested and detained.

So much for the UK being the protectors of free speech.

Sean grabbed Mrs Foog's hand tight. "You have to leave now. You will be arrested,"

The woman laughed. "Then let them arrest me for protesting against them. This might not be a free country anymore but I intend to get revenge for my husband one way or another,"

Sean smiled. He really liked this woman.

Harry stepped forward. "Names?"

The woman nodded. "There was one name he kept repeating again and again,"

Sean heard the professional policing students

laugh as the constables pushed a part the crowds and arrested the daughter and the son.

Then a constable grabbed the mother.

"Ariana Smith," the woman shouted.

The constable charged through the crowd towards Sean and Harry.

He grabbed Harry and they ran.

He had to tell auntie what he knew and he had to get to the truth.

And he had to find a way to help Mrs Foog get out of prison for just protesting peacefully. But that was firmly in the hands of his wonderful auntie.

CHAPTER 13
10th November 2023
Canterbury, England

Bettie was rather surprised as she went down into the massive circular reception of the hospital with its awful grey plain walls, huge wooden desk with computers on it in the middle and hundreds of different doors leading off to different wards.

Bettie looked at a very tall business-like looking woman who was sitting on a rose of wooden chairs set against the furthest wall, she had to be Victoria but it was the two people at the reception area that was concerning her.

It was a man and a woman. They were both wearing black trousers, white shirts and black shoes. They almost looked like twins except for the woman had a very short blond haircut but the man had longish brown hair.

Bettie went over to them and sexy Graham went round the other side so if they tried to escape they could grab the detectives.

"Bettie English private eye and president of the Federation," she said extending her hand.

The man rolled his eyes. "You are interfering with a police investigation,"

Bettie nodded at the three women in blue nurses' uniforms who sat behind the desk to tell them that everything was okay.

"Shall we take a seat?" Graham asked.

The woman shook her head. "We have a dangerous suspect to interview,"

"That's weird, isn't it Graham?" Bettie asked. "Considering Kinsley is in a coma and cannot be spoken to at this time. What are you really after?"

The man smiled.

He threw a punch.

Bettie dodged it.

Grabbed the man's wrist.

Pulling it behind his back.

Slamming his body against the desk.

The three nurses tried to reassure a group of patients as they walked past.

"That wasn't very nice," Bettie said in the man's ear. "Who are you? What do you want?"

"I am Detective Ellis Callum of Kent Police and you have just assaulted a police officer,"

"We both know this hospital has excellent cameras. It will be easy to prove that you assault me first and I did this in self-defence. Tell me what I want to know,"

Bettie looked at the woman who Graham had in a head hold. "Do you want to tell me?"

She shook her head, or as much as Graham would allow her.

"You have until the count of three to tell me about the Cabal or I am performing a citizen's arrest and marching you down to a police station and filing charges,"

"Nothing will happen," the woman said.

Bettie nodded because that was true. "But I will then go on the news tonight and report to all my journalist friends about your little Cabal. Then the entire nation will focus on your little group,"

Bettie felt Ellis swallow hard.

"Do you not like that Mr Callum?"

"She's going to kill my family," Ellis said.

The woman grinned.

She stomped on Graham's foot.

He released her.

She flew at Bettie.

Tackling her to the floor.

Bettie blocked three punches.

The woman pinned her down.

She whipped out a Glock.

Victoria smashed the woman over the head.

The gun flew through the air.

Graham carefully caught it.

Victoria took out handcuffs and put them on the woman.

Bettie frowned at Ellis. "What's going on here?"

Ellis started to cry but Bettie shot him a warning look. "A great friend of mine is in a coma, I was almost killed twice in a single fucking day and I want to see my kids tonight,"

Ellis nodded. "The Cabal isn't actually five people. It's one woman who has four people working for her, she's very cold, very clever and makes your Article 20 and 66 look like nothing,"

Bettie laughed. If that was true then the silly little man had no idea what he was talking about since Article 20 and 66 of the Private Eye Act (2022) were the Federation's blackmail articles that could annihilate governments, institutions and everything in between by exposing all their corruption all over the world from 1918 onwards.

She doubted this Cabal woman could have done the same in that time.

"Who is she?" Bettie asked.

"I don't know. She has my wife and I've seen photos of my daughter on her university campus. She's watching her," Ellis said.

Bettie looked at Graham and he nodded. She completely agreed, she didn't believe he was lying for a single moment but there was clearly a lot of blackmail happening at the moment.

They still needed to know what was happening with Granger and Bettie really wanted to know how Sean was getting on but right now she needed to know what the plan was.

"The plan for Kinsley what was it?" Graham

asked just a moment before she could.

Ellis shook his head and passed Bettie a syringe. "I don't know what it contains but I needed to inject this into him or my wife and daughter die today,"

Bettie weakly smiled as she passed it over to Fran as she entered the reception. "Get this to the Federation labs immediately put an extra-rush on it. We need to know what resources our foes have as soon as possible,"

Fran nodded as she quickly left.

Bettie went over to Victoria and the woman as she started to regain consciousness. "Take her away and I want to know exactly who she is,"

"Of course," Victoria said.

Bettie hoped Neil's security company had accessed to similar databases as they did when it came to fingerprints.

Bettie's phone buzzed and she agreed as Sean had done his job perfectly. He was such a great kid.

"We need to talk to Ariana Smith immediately," Bettie said.

CHAPTER 14
10th November 2023
Canterbury, England

Graham pulled into Ariana's gravel driveaway with Bettie next to him and he just turned off the car without getting out. Bettie had been doing some research on her on the way over but he still didn't like this. If he was still a cop then he could have easily called in back-up, tactical response or anything else that he needed to deal with a potential shooter.

He hated all of this.

Graham couldn't deny that Arianna had a great two-storey semi-detached house with excellent red trimming around the windows, a black plastic front door with a really nice glass decorative feature that he couldn't see completely in the darkness and Graham noticed that the red curtains weren't drawn.

A little odd considering how the sky was black with no moon or stars out tonight and Graham forced himself not to take that as a warning that something bad was about to happen. He looked around as the light from Bettie's phone lit up her beautiful face, there was no one about, no other cars on the road and there weren't even any dog walkers.

The entire street was eerily silent and Graham just couldn't help but feel like something bad was about to happen.

Graham stepped out the car with Bettie close behind him.

"Arianna has been a detective for five years and has worked on plenty of major cases and her known boyfriend works for tactical response," Bettie said.

"That would explain the firearms,"

Graham went over to the front door and went to knock on it but the door was already open.

An icy cold gust blew past them and the door swung wide open.

Just in case this was part of a setup, Graham took out his phone and started recording.

"This is former Detective Graham Adams at the house of suspect Arianna Smith, we have just arrived at 18:00 door is open. Going inside,"

Graham popped his phone in his top pocket and allowed the camera to keep rolling. It would be annoying as hell if anyone claimed he had broken in, but he knew Bettie *might* have done that already on previous cases.

"This is really fun breaking into places," Bettie said knowing it would annoy him. "I do this a lot on cases,"

Graham smiled and kept on walking into the house. He was going along a long white corridor with a living room and bathroom to the left, the stairs in front of him at the very end and a small guest room to his right.

Graham went through the huge perfectly clean living room and he went into a bright white modern kitchen but he hated what he saw on the floor.

He shook his head as he saw the cold, bloody and very dead corpse of Arianna Smith.

Graham took out his phone and kept filming whilst Bettie went over and checked for a pulse.

"She's dead and still lukewarm like a bad cup of tea," Bettie said.

Graham playfully hit her on the head. He couldn't believe she had just said that about a dead person.

"Graham she was a corrupt cop. She deserved that comment,"

"What evidence?"

Bettie laughed and pointed to her necklace, watch and bracelets. Graham smiled, they were all made from 24-carat gold and he was pretty sure the diamonds in them were all real.

"Come on Graham," Bettie said. "We're millionaires and I wouldn't even buy this stuff. I prefer to help charities than waste money on this crap,"

Graham kissed her on the head. He loved her so damn much.

He knelt down next to Arianna and looked around. There was a small bullet hole in her chest, a different bullet than the ones recovered at Gabby's murder but two dead cops in a single day.

Whoever this Cabal was had to be trying to tidy up any loose ends.

Graham stopped the recording and called Sean. Harry answered immediately and Graham heard cars in the background so Sean had to be the one driving.

"Harry," Graham said, "need you to look up those police constables you mentioned that arrested the protesters. Did any one of them make a strange call to someone possibly in the cabal?"

The line went silent for a moment.

"Yes," Harry said, "two minutes after we outrun the constable chasing us. All three of them made a phone call to Arianna Smith,"

"Probably about the name you gave us," Bettie said.

Graham put the call on speaker. "It makes no sense but we would have forced the killer's hand. Who was with Arianna at the time of the call to make them feel like they had no other choice than to kill her?"

"That is something I intend to find out," Granger said.

Graham and Bettie stood up and a group of constables and Granger placed handcuffs on them and Granger read out the formal caution as they were taken out of the house, put into police cars and taken away.

Graham knew something bad was going to happen. Why hadn't he listened?

CHAPTER 15
10th November 2023
Maidstone, England

Bettie sat on an awfully warm black plastic chair in the middle of a small kitchenette at the massive Maidstone police station with its awful grey walls, orange floor and it seriously looked like it was from the last century. It was simply awful.

The smell of burnt "coffee", mouldy teabags and rotting food was disgusting. She couldn't believe normal police officers actually worked like this.

"Miss English," Inspector Granger said walking in and offering her a mug of "coffee" that she very quickly declined. "I know you did not kill Arianna but I need to question you anyway,"

As much as Bettie wanted to ask about Graham, she knew he was a cop first and foremost. He would tell them everything they wanted to know no matter what she wanted, he still believed in the perfection and idealism of the police.

Granger sat down on a black plastic chair opposite her. It cracked under his weight but Bettie wanted to believe it was because of the age of the chairs and definitely not his weight.

"What did you find?" Bettie asked.

"I'm asking the questions here and just be grateful I don't have you in a simple interview room,"

"Maybe you should reconsider that opinion," Bettie said knowing she was about to cross a line. "Considering an interview would be taped and I could say on record how you got rid of a memory stick,"

Granger's face paled.

"We know from police evidence logs that a memory stick that I took pictures on was never entered into evidence. Why?"

Granger looked around and Bettie enjoyed seeing him panic.

"We also know that your daughter's pending drunken disorderly warning was removed from police databases," Bettie said deciding it was a good idea to risk a lie. "But not before we could take a photo of the now-missing charge,"

Granger's face went paler and paler like he was dying. Maybe he was inside but Bettie didn't care, her friend was in a coma and Granger was enabling his attackers to escape.

"Tell me what I want to know or I will post on social media that you're a dirty cop,"

Granger frowned. "My daughter's amazing you know. She's going to graduate top of her class in July and she wants to follow my footsteps but she was drunk one night. She punched a cop,"

Bettie didn't dare react just in case that silenced him.

"I managed to get the constable to drop it down to a drunken disorderly but it was common knowledge what she had done. And... and I just wanted to help my daughter with a clean record,"

Bettie could understand that, she would have done anything to help Elizabeth but Granger had still committed a crime.

"I still have the stick if you want it," Granger said weakly smiling passing it over to her.

Bettie smiled as she held the small silver memory stick in her hand because this was the proof that Kinsley had wanted to give her late last night and after 24 hours she finally had it.

"Will you, you know, end my career?" Granger asked.

Bettie was surprised at how sheepish and weak he looked, and as much as she didn't want to admit it, she knew he was just a scared man doing whatever he could for his daughter.

He was a family man at heart and damn it, Bettie couldn't hurt him or his career. Not that he needed to know that.

"Answer my questions then," Bettie said. "How did the blackmailer contact you?"

"She spoke to me through Arianna Smith. Arianna came over to me one day and passed me a phone, on the other end was the Cabal that's what she called herself. She offered me the chance to help my daughter in exchange for the memory stick,"

"And where were you meant to meet her?"

Granger laughed. "At Arianna's house so I went with three constables to arrest her and the Cabal for daring to threaten me but that's when I found you,"

Bettie nodded. She finally knew who was with Arianna and had killed her.

"Is there anything you can tell me about the Cabal?"

Granger took a massive sip of the "coffee". "No she's a woman. No accent so comes from the area and she didn't want to talk about anything besides the police. There was a noise though in the background like a helicopter or something taking off or landing above her. I don't know,"

Bettie didn't know many places that had helipads but she wanted to find out.

Granger started coughing.

He foamed around the mouth.

Bettie called for help.

She called 999.

She swore as Granger gasped for air.

CHAPTER 16
10th November 2023
Canterbury, England

Graham was so damn annoyed at this damn Cabal woman, how dare she attack Kinsley, kill Arianna and Gabby and now Granger was at the hospital having his stomach pumped free of the poison. He was so glad that Bettie was okay and hadn't drunk any of the "coffee" offered to her.

As soon as they had gotten back from picking up the kids from Bettie's mum's they had come back, read them a quick story before kissing them and putting them to bed.

Graham loved family time.

He hugged Bettie as they all sat on the large black sofas with Harry, Sean and Fran sitting on the other black sofa next to them. They all needed to find answers because he just wasn't sure they would make it through the night at the rate the Cabal's woman was going.

Sean connected his laptop to a small projector and smiled as he finished sorting out the memory stick.

"Auntie the stick needs your face to be unlocked,"

Graham was impressed. Kinsley really had thought of everything.

Bettie went over to Sean's laptop and as soon as the laptop camera saw her, Graham was amazed as screenshots and photos of tens upon tens of documents showed up.

They all started reading the documents off the projector and he couldn't believe what he was reading. They were all reading emails, official requests and cases going back five years.

Graham focused on emails about getting rid of incorruptible officers, removing critics of police stop and search and police *roughening up* and there was even an email about links between the members of the Cabal and the KKK.

He had no idea what the hell this Cabal was up to but this was messed up.

Then Graham started to notice that everything came back to a single name that was repeated over and over again. It was on all the emails, all the requests and the photos of meet-ups all showed a very small, fit woman.

Rachel Andrews.

Graham had heard the name before, he just couldn't place it but if even half of this was true then

Graham wasn't sure how Kent Police would ever recover and as much as he didn't like the Cabal. He knew they couldn't expose all of this.

Especially as Sean clicked on one document outlining how the Cabal wanted her four "Underservants" to frame a police Inspector for an assault because he was getting too close to the truth and the method of the sexual assault was beyond horrific.

He was dealing with a monster. The only comfort he got from the document was that the Cabal said it couldn't be real.

But the Inspector's career was still over anyway.

"Miss Andrews is…" Fran said her voice shaking towards the end.

"What?" Graham asked.

"She isn't a cop. She was one but she was fired five years ago for police brutality and the murder of a black student,"

Graham's felt his stomach twist. "How the hell is the bastard not in prison?"

Fran weakly smiled. "Administrative error resulted in the footage showing the assault disappeared,"

"Bullshit," Sean said.

Graham looked at Bettie. This was serious now because they finally had their killer, they just had to prove it. And as much as Graham wanted to say he was impartial and knew what to do, he didn't. He couldn't believe some idiot was trying to destroy the police force he loved so much.

"This is proof," Harry said.

"But it isn't enough," Bettie said. "This proves corruption and a shit load of it but this doesn't get justice for Kinsley, Gabby and Arianna,"

Sean played around on his laptop a little. "There's proof on here too about the four Underservants. Arianna's one and then there are three more names,"

Graham tapped Bettie on the shoulder. "And remember why Kinsley wanted to come here in the first place. He didn't trust the police to deal with this properly,"

Harry shook his head. "What if he actually didn't know what to do?"

Graham smiled. "Of course. This memory stick shows tons of corruption that would destroy Kent Police just like how the Met in London is crippled for good reason,"

"And Kinsley still believed in the police," Bettie said.

"So do I," Graham said realising he actually meant that for the first time in ages.

"He wanted to know what he should do," Bettie said, "and that's why I want Rachel Andrews on charges of murder and not corruption,"

"Expose the murder the corruption goes away and Kent Police is safe," Graham said.

"And we can use the corruption evidence as proof and leverage for another time," Sean said.

"But the question is," Fran said, "how do we get a woman who's established such a great network, for murder?"

Graham smiled at the woman he loved because that really was the million-dollar question.

CHAPTER 17
10th November 2023
Canterbury, England

Bettie loved the great thick aroma of bitter coffee (the real stuff compared to the police crap), crispy bacon and sweet vanilla pastries as Fran returned from the kitchen and Bettie slid onto the floor.

Sean joined her with his laptop and Bettie was more than determined to figure out exactly what was happening here, but there was no way in hell she was allowing all this evidence about Kent Police corruption to get out.

They would annihilate the police and way too many great officers would have their careers obliterated because of a bad few.

"The phone call that Arianna gave Granger," Bettie said.

Sean pulled it up on his laptop. "Here it came from a burner phone,"

Bettie checked the list of names of the three

other Underservants and found the name of Arianna's boyfriend.

"Okay so Rachel calls Arianna's boyfriend to do the hit and kill Gabby so that explains that," Bettie said.

Bettie smiled as Fran passed her a large vanilla pastry. She loved the stickiness of the icing on her fingers.

"Then a detective Elliot Nelson was at the station when Granger was poisoned so he probably poisoned him," Harry said.

"And," Fran said, "the woman Victoria arrested at the hospital. She was at the police college with Rachel,"

Bettie was so glad to finally know what these corrupt officers were doing and what they had done to the victims. It still didn't explain what had happened to Kinsley and sadly none of it could be tied back to Rachel.

"Can we round them up?" Bettie asked.

"No, I'm, not a cop anymore," Graham said.

Bettie didn't like that. She wanted a lead, a real one so she took out her phone and called the Federation contractor that had been running the tests for her.

She put it on speaker.

"Any results Jase?" Bettie asked.

The man on the other end of the phone laughed. "Of course Miss English, we have results for the syringe you gave us,"

"I won't bother telling you the name of the toxin because it is basically bleach. Not very clever or sophisticated so I think this was a rushed job. It was a normal everyday household bleach too,"

"Any fingerprints?"

"None at all besides Ellis',"

Bettie thanked him and hung up but then her phone started ringing straight after from Zoey.

"Bettie I've finished running the tests on Gabby's shooting because of a very thinly veiled threat from the Chief Constable. I found a print on one of the shell casings,"

"Let me ask it belongs to a former cop by the name of Rachel Andrews,"

"It is but that's not why I'm calling. I pinged her phone after getting a warrant and she's walking up your road. I'm sending back up and you need to be careful,"

Bettie was about to say something when static filled the line.

Bettie smiled at the family she loved and they all nodded. They all knew they were going to have to be careful here and they had to stop a cold blooded killer from finishing them off.

Something that excited her a lot more than she ever wanted to admit.

CHAPTER 18
10th November 2023
Canterbury, England

Rachel Andrews stood outside Bettie's large detached house and it was rather nice she supposed. The front door was as black as night like her heart and all the neighbours were out or not daring to look outside at that late night.

Rachel liked that about people.

The air was cold like her and the awful aroma of damp, freshly cut grass and mint filled the air. Rachel didn't know why someone would cut their grass in November but that wasn't her problem.

Bettie English was her problem.

She stood in front of the front door in her mother's military tactical gear and with two semi-automatic rifles in her hands. She had admired Bettie English for a long time but now she was just a pain in the ass.

If Bettie hadn't interfered so much in her plans

then maybe she would have lived a little longer or maybe she would have died quickly. But Rachel wanted Bettie to die slowly and painfully just so Bettie could understand the pain she was causing Rachel right now.

It was a shame that officers like Graham couldn't understand that once the police had been such a powerful force for good. They could get rid of the criminal blacks, beat up the youth and criminals without a second thought and the police could shoot whatever Islamic terrorist they wanted.

But things were different.

All those sissy liberal laws had crippled the police and now crime was the highest it had been in human history and Rachel was on a mission to make the police great again.

And all that would start and be a lot easier once Bettie English and her interfering family was dead.

Something they would all be in a matter of minutes.

CHAPTER 19
10th November 2023
Canterbury, England

Bettie turned off all the lights as she gripped a small frying pan (a trick she had learnt from her best friend Zoey) and she crouched behind one of the black sofas they had pulled out.

She knew that Rachel was only after her to stop her from investigating so Bettie wasn't concerned about anyone else in the house, but Rachel was clearly crazy so she was going to have to be careful.

The front door smashed open.

Bettie didn't dare breathe and she just looked at the black shadow next to her that was Graham and Fran. Even the outside streetlights did nothing to lighten up the living room.

Harry and Sean were hiding in the kitchen in a move to hopefully ambush Rachel but Bettie wanted something first. She wanted a confession so she turned on the recorder on her phone.

The heavy footsteps of Rachel entering the house echoed around the living room.

Bettie was grateful she was good at throwing her voice nowadays so it wasn't clear where she was when she spoke.

"What do you want?" Bettie asked.

Rachel laughed and Bettie heard her enter the living room.

"To make the police great again," Rachel said.

Bettie hated how dark and evil she sounded.

"Did you know when my father was young and he was a cop the police were respected? When someone in the streets was a cop they were bowed down to,"

Bettie hated this woman as she heard Rachel stand in the doorway.

"But look at the police now. The media, the public and the politicians all roasting the police alive. It is a disgusting reality considering how heroic the police are. I want to change that,"

"You want people to fear you," Sean said.

Bettie swore under her breath. It was easy to tell he was in the kitchen that would bring Rachel straight past them.

Rachel laughed. "You must be the fag that my research showed up. My father killed some of your kind and I would be happy to continue the tradition,"

Bettie swallowed hard as she heard Rachel reload her guns.

"You cannot get away with this," Bettie said.

Rachel fired into the other sofa.

Fran screamed.

Bettie rolled her eyes as Rachel stopped.

"It was worth a try to see where you were hiding," Rachal said.

Bettie prepared to pounce.

A smoke grenade smashed on Graham's head.

Bettie shot out into the open.

She spun around.

She looked at Rachel's shadowy outline.

Rachel raised her guns.

Smoke filled the room.

Bettie threw the frying pan.

It missed.

Rachel fired.

Gunshots filled the air.

Bettie dived to one side.

A frying pan hit something.

Bettie rolled her eyes.

Bloody Fran or Graham probably hit each other by mistake.

Bullets screamed through the air.

The smoke got thicker.

Bettie's eyes burnt.

Someone punched her in the stomach.

The smoke cleared.

Bettie felt someone climb on top of her.

Rachel rammed the guns into Bettie's head.

"Investigating crime is a man's job you feminist nazi," Rachel said.

Bettie laughed. "That's rich coming from you a former detective,"

Rachel hesitated.

Bettie whacked Rachel round the face.

She fell off Bettie.

Bettie jumped her.

Rachel kicked her legs out from under her.

Rachel climbed on Bettie's leg.

Bettie heard the click of a gun.

And a whack of a frying pan hitting Rachel's head.

"Take that homophobic bitch," Sean said.

Bettie laughed and went over and switched on the lights to just shake her head at a passed-out Graham and Fran.

She couldn't believe her two stupid idiots that she really loved had panicked and hit each other on the head by accident.

They were stupid at times but she loved them more than anything else in the world.

And the best thing was, little Harrison and Elizabeth had slept through the entire thing. That was a great achievement in Bettie's eyes and the criminals had been caught but this was still far from over.

CHAPTER 20
13th November 2023
Maidstone, England

Graham was really grateful that the Chief Detective Inspector now running the investigation had allowed him and Bettie to sit in his rather nice office with glass walls, a large brown messy desk and three very old wooden chairs to watch the interview of Rachel Andrews.

Graham couldn't deny that he was a little scared to move because he was sure the wooden chairs were so old they were going to break at any moment, but he forced himself to move every so often so his joints didn't ache.

He was surprised at the sheer lack of activity in the bullpen outside the glass walls of the office. There were rows upon rows of white plastic desks covered in all sorts of rubbish, files and computers but so few cops sat at them.

There were a few very thin and green cops that

were probably in their first month on the job sitting around an older detective's desk but there were no more nor no less.

Graham really liked the sweet rose, jasmine and lilac scents that came off sexy Bettie's hair and he so badly wanted to kiss her especially after listening to all the outrageous things that Rachel had been saying about how the police had fallen.

It was awful to imagine that Rachel had brainwashed herself into believing all those lies. He didn't have the heart to tell her all the disgusting things her father's generation of cops used to do with the women in the dark, lonely, isolated prison cells.

She wouldn't listen.

But at least she had confessed to everything from ordering Arianna's boyfriend to killing Gabby to another detective Underservant of attacking Kinsley and another one poisoning Granger.

And she had confessed to killing Arianna herself.

All her underservants had already been brought in and they were saying the same crap as her but they were all arrested, charged and they would be going away for a very, very long time.

A small group of detectives in shirts and jeans came into the bullpen with a thief that Graham recognised from the Most Wanted emails he used to get every morning.

Other officers cheered him but as much as Graham didn't want to admit it, he just didn't feel alive in this place anymore. He knew it sounded rubbish even to himself but when he was a newish cop he used to love coming in, seeing the other officers and working cases.

He still loved working cases, helping people and making a difference. Yet the police just wasn't for him anymore.

It killed him to even admit that but it was only now he was realising how true it was.

Graham had spent years, decades even standing up for his fellow officers against sexism, racism and homophobia but the problem was bigger than that. The police were just institutionally all those things and the people in charge absolutely didn't want to change and that was Graham's problem.

Especially as not once had a fellow police officer ever had his back when the top-brass or corrupted officers tried to get rid of him.

Why should he work for an organisation that fundamentally hated him? And it wasn't like the other cops even tried to hide their hatred of him.

A few moments later Graham was surprised to see Chief Constable Jordan walk in wearing his full official police uniform. Graham shook his greasy hand as he sat behind the desk and he placed Graham's badge on the desk.

Graham looked at Bettie and she gave him an all-knowing smile. Damn he loved her so much, she was just so clever, wonderful and understanding.

"One of the so-called Underservants confessed to monitoring the hospital systems by hacking the hospital so it was him that called Jason as soon as Kinsley was admitted," the Chief Constable said.

Graham nodded. That was good news at least.

"What happened to Granger's wife and daughter?" Bettie asked.

"The wife was found safe and sound at Rachel's house. She was kept in the shed and she's at the hospital now. The daughter had no any idea about what was happening but she's with her mother now,"

"Good," Graham said. "What about the protesters?"

Jordan sneered. "My constables thought there was a chance the protest would turn disruptive so they acted. The protest is illegal anyway,"

Graham laughed. "Oh no someone is protesting they must be criminals. How dare someone point out the flaws in the police. The sheer horror,"

"Are you done?" Jordan asked.

Graham smiled and shrugged. "The law is stupid and you know it. People should be allowed to protest peacefully and that is exactly what the mother and children of Derrick Foog were doing,"

Bettie leant closer. "Tell me Chief Constable what would happen if I called my good friend Skylar Mason, the Justice Secretary and asked her to look into your position,"

Jordan frowned. "I'll release the protesters tomorrow and I'll recant the charges,"

"Today," Bettie said.

"Fine,"

Graham loved Bettie. She was flat out amazing.

"What is Kent Police going to do about all policies and Misconduct Hearings that the Cabal influenced?" Bettie asked.

Jordan smiled. "Each one will be reevaluated in light of new evidence and-"

Graham waved him silent. "We all know in the end that nothing will change,"

"Of course not," Jordan said. "I would rather focus rather on putting criminals away than focusing on Woke bullshit about how to increase blacks in the police force,"

Graham laughed. "Do you realise all that Woke means is your aware inequality exists in the world? Woke doesn't mean anything else and it isn't a bad thing,"

Jordan shrugged. "I have actual police work to do Detective Adams. I want you back first thing on Monday,"

Bettie stood up. "We both know the evidence Kinsley obtained is more than enough to annihilate this police force,"

Jordan swallowed hard. "What do you want?"

Graham stood up and put a loving arm around Bettie.

"Nothing," Bettie said. "The Federation will add this evidence to our Blackmail Articles so just, be careful about what you do in the future. I have no problem destroying you if you bully minorities and other innocent people,"

"Idiots," Jordan said as he walked away.

"I resign!" Graham shouted.

Jordan stopped dead in his tracks and Graham followed him out of the office so everyone could hear what he had to say.

Enough was enough.

"I have had enough of this police force that is racist, sexist and homophobic at its very heart. I am the only police officer it feels like that wants to stand up for everyone,"

Everyone looked at Graham.

"No one else challenges the sexist jokes we hear in the kitchen or toilets. No one else challenges the racism we encounter in the bullpen when we're searching for suspects. No one else challenges the homophobia we face when a hate crime call comes in,"

Everyone frowned at Graham.

"There are some amazing officers in this force I have worked with so many of you and I loved it. But I will no longer work for a police force that never supports me in turn,"

Graham looked at Bettie and he smiled as she looked like a very proud mother.

Something he really loved about her and as they both went out of the police station hand in hand, he couldn't deny that the future was uncertain because he was no longer a cop and he had no idea what he was besides from a cop. But what he did know with all his heart was that his future was going to be amazing as long as he had his children, his family and most importantly the sexy woman he loved by his side.

Something he knew he would always have and he would always be grateful for those most important things.

CHAPTER 21
17th November 2023
Canterbury, England

Bettie was so excited as she stood in the wonderfully warm hospital room belonging to Kinsley because the doctors had brought him out of the medically induced coma and they said he should be waking up at any moment.

It was so great to have everyone here and Bettie was really glad that Granger had been released and he had given her a thousand pounds as payment for finding out who had poisoned him. And the Foog family had paid her the same amount as a thank you.

Bettie leant against the warm grey wall of Kinsley's room and smiled as Sean and Harry and Graham all leant over Kinsley's hospital bed waiting for the precious moment when he finally woke up. Bettie had to admit how cute Sean and Harry looked as they held his hands and they were such a brilliant couple.

And even though she knew they could always hold their own against the haters, she was always going to protect them no matter what. Sean was legally her own child anyway but both of them were her family and she loved them both.

Little Harrison and Elizabeth were chasing each other round Neil as he sat on the floor with Fran, and Bettie took some photos of them on her phone because all of them were so cute.

And Bettie felt relieved to discover what had happened and now the world was certainly a safer place. Of course the world would never ever know that the Cabal existed but the proof that Kinsley gave her was safely tucked away in Article 20 and 66 of the Federation.

It was perfect blackmail material anyway in case Kent Police went after anyone she loved with all their might. Something she knew would never happen.

And Bettie was really glad that she had spoken to Gabby's ex-husband and kids just yesterday and explained to the kids that their mother truly, truly loved her. Then Bettie had forced the husband to pay her a hundred thousand pounds as shush money so she didn't tell the court that he had made up lies about Gabby to get full custody.

Bettie would just use the money anyway for her charities, and she made the husband promise her that he would always make sure the kids remembered their mother for the amazing woman she was.

Gabby just might have been dead but at least she

might have got her wish about her kids at least knowing of her again.

It was a small victory.

"Welcome back!" Graham shouted hugging Kinsley.

Bettie felt a wave of emotion wash over her as Kinsley awoke and hugged all three of them and then Neil and Fran hugged him too.

"Mummy," Elizabeth asked, "where's juice please?"

"Good girl," Bettie said as she passed Elizabeth a little bottle of juice.

Bettie went over to Kinsley and she was surprised by how much he was grinning at her.

"Did you do it?"

Bettie nodded. "The Cabal is gone and the evidence is safely away in the Articles. You're a hero,"

Kinsley shrugged but his face twisted into agony. "I don't know about that but I knew you would know what to do,"

Bettie smiled, glided past Graham and she kissed Kinsley's forehead. "We're both heroes then,"

Kinsley nodded and then Graham started talking to him about everything that had happened.

And Bettie sort of just fell against the wooden chair in the far corner of the hospital room and she felt numb for a moment.

Her beautiful, sexy Graham wasn't a cop anymore. He was unemployed and she didn't mind that, she really didn't but she knew that it would eat away and kill Graham over time.

He was a cop through and through and he was so passionate about being a cop that she wasn't sure he would love or even enjoy any other job.

But she was the President of the British Private Eye Federation and that meant she had power, Bettie had no idea how she was going to fix this or help Graham get another job in the police in some capacity, but she would because she loved him.

And it was tomorrow's problem anyway.

Bettie stood up and went over to Kinsley's bed and joined in the conversations they were having about the Cabal, about love and about family and Bettie didn't have a single problem with those beautiful topics because she loved them all and her children especially.

"Mummy!" Harrison shouted.

Bettie laughed as she looked at Elizabeth holding her bottle without a lid on it as she had just thrown the juice over Harrison exactly like he had done to her a week ago.

"Payback," Elizabeth said.

Bettie just kissed her children and hugged them tight. They really were the most precious thing in the entire world and she would always love them no matter what.

GET YOUR FREE SHORT STORY NOW! And get signed up to Connor Whiteley's newsletter to hear about new gripping books, offers and exciting projects. (You'll never be sent spam)
https://www.subscribepage.com/wintersignup

About the author:

Connor Whiteley is the author of over 60 books in the sci-fi fantasy, nonfiction psychology and books for writer's genre and he is a Human Branding Speaker and Consultant.

He is a passionate warhammer 40,000 reader, psychology student and author.

Who narrates his own audiobooks and he hosts The Psychology World Podcast.

All whilst studying Psychology at the University of Kent, England.

Also, he was a former Explorer Scout where he gave a speech to the Maltese President in August 2018 and he attended Prince Charles' 70th Birthday Party at Buckingham Palace in May 2018.

Plus, he is a self-confessed coffee lover!

Other books by Connor Whiteley:

Bettie English Private Eye Series

A Very Private Woman
The Russian Case
A Very Urgent Matter
A Case Most Personal
Trains, Scots and Private Eyes
The Federation Protects
Cops, Robbers and Private Eyes
Just Ask Bettie English
An Inheritance To Die For
The Death of Graham Adams
Bearing Witness
The Twelve
The Wrong Body
The Assassination Of Bettie English
Wining And Dying
Eight Hours
Uniformed Cabal
A Case Most Christmas

Gay Romance Novellas

Breaking, Nursing, Repairing A Broken Heart
Jacob And Daniel
Fallen For A Lie
Spying And Weddings
Clean Break
Awakening Love
Meeting A Country Man
Loving Prime Minister

Snowed In Love
Never Been Kissed
Love Betrays You

<u>Lord of War Origin Trilogy:</u>
Not Scared Of The Dark
Madness
Burn Them All

<u>The Fireheart Fantasy Series</u>
Heart of Fire
Heart of Lies
Heart of Prophecy
Heart of Bones
Heart of Fate

<u>City of Assassins (Urban Fantasy)</u>
City of Death
City of Marytrs
City of Pleasure
City of Power

<u>Agents of The Emperor</u>
Return of The Ancient Ones
Vigilance
Angels of Fire
Kingmaker
The Eight
The Lost Generation
Hunt

Emperor's Council
Speaker of Treachery
Birth Of The Empire
Terraforma
Spaceguard

<u>The Rising Augusta Fantasy Adventure Series</u>
Rise To Power
Rising Walls
Rising Force
Rising Realm

<u>Lord Of War Trilogy (Agents of The Emperor)</u>
Not Scared Of The Dark
Madness
Burn It All Down

<u>Miscellaneous:</u>
RETURN
FREEDOM
SALVATION
Reflection of Mount Flame
The Masked One
The Great Deer
English Independence

OTHER SHORT STORIES BY CONNOR WHITELEY

<u>Mystery Short Story Collections</u>

Criminally Good Stories Volume 1: 20 Detective Mystery Short Stories

Criminally Good Stories Volume 2: 20 Private Investigator Short Stories

Criminally Good Stories Volume 3: 20 Crime Fiction Short Stories

Criminally Good Stories Volume 4: 20 Science Fiction and Fantasy Mystery Short Stories

Criminally Good Stories Volume 5: 20 Romantic Suspense Short Stories

<u>Mystery Short Stories:</u>

Protecting The Woman She Hated

Finding A Royal Friend

Our Woman In Paris

Corrupt Driving

A Prime Assassination

Jubilee Thief

Jubilee, Terror, Celebrations

Negative Jubilation

Ghostly Jubilation

Killing For Womenkind

A Snowy Death

Miracle Of Death

A Spy In Rome

The 12:30 To St Pancreas

A Country In Trouble

A Smokey Way To Go
A Spicy Way To GO
A Marketing Way To Go
A Missing Way To Go
A Showering Way To Go
Poison In The Candy Cane
Kendra Detective Mystery Collection Volume 1
Kendra Detective Mystery Collection Volume 2
Mystery Short Story Collection Volume 1
Mystery Short Story Collection Volume 2
Criminal Performance
Candy Detectives
Key To Birth In The Past

Science Fiction Short Stories:
Their Brave New World
Gummy Bear Detective
The Candy Detective
What Candies Fear
The Blurred Image
Shattered Legions
The First Rememberer
Life of A Rememberer
System of Wonder
Lifesaver
Remarkable Way She Died
The Interrogation of Annabella Stormic
Blade of The Emperor
Arbiter's Truth
Computation of Battle

Old One's Wrath
Puppets and Masters
Ship of Plague
Interrogation
Edge of Failure

<u>Fantasy Short Stories:</u>
City of Snow
City of Light
City of Vengeance
Dragons, Goats and Kingdom
Smog The Pathetic Dragon
Don't Go In The Shed
The Tomato Saver
The Remarkable Way She Died
Dragon Coins
Dragon Tea
Dragon Rider

All books in 'An Introductory Series':

Careers In Psychology

Psychology of Suicide

Dementia Psychology

Clinical Psychology Reflections Volume 4

Forensic Psychology of Terrorism And Hostage-Taking

Forensic Psychology of False Allegations

Year In Psychology

CBT For Anxiety

CBT For Depression

Applied Psychology

BIOLOGICAL PSYCHOLOGY 3RD EDITION

COGNITIVE PSYCHOLOGY THIRD EDITION

SOCIAL PSYCHOLOGY- 3RD EDITION

ABNORMAL PSYCHOLOGY 3RD EDITION

PSYCHOLOGY OF RELATIONSHIPS- 3RD EDITION

DEVELOPMENTAL PSYCHOLOGY 3RD EDITION

HEALTH PSYCHOLOGY

RESEARCH IN PSYCHOLOGY

A GUIDE TO MENTAL HEALTH AND TREATMENT AROUND THE WORLD- A GLOBAL LOOK AT DEPRESSION

FORENSIC PSYCHOLOGY

THE FORENSIC PSYCHOLOGY OF THEFT, BURGLARY AND OTHER CRIMES AGAINST PROPERTY

CRIMINAL PROFILING: A FORENSIC

PSYCHOLOGY GUIDE TO FBI PROFILING AND GEOGRAPHICAL AND STATISTICAL PROFILING.
CLINICAL PSYCHOLOGY FORMULATION IN PSYCHOTHERAPY
PERSONALITY PSYCHOLOGY AND INDIVIDUAL DIFFERENCES
CLINICAL PSYCHOLOGY REFLECTIONS VOLUME 1
CLINICAL PSYCHOLOGY REFLECTIONS VOLUME 2
Clinical Psychology Reflections Volume 3
CULT PSYCHOLOGY
Police Psychology

A Psychology Student's Guide To University
How Does University Work?
A Student's Guide To University And Learning
University Mental Health and Mindset